# The Great Train Race
## THE DAY TROTTIN' SALLY BEAT
## THE CAROLINA SPECIAL

Told by Johnny Thomas Fowler
Illustrated by Raymond L Floyd 3/7/24

*Johny Thomas Fowler*

## Hairy Toe Productions

# For my son
# Taylor

Printed and bound in the USA by
Createspace an Amazon Company
illustrations by Raymond L. Floyd
Color correction by Cecil J. William
Graphic Design and layout by John Thomas Fowler
The artwork was funded in part by  The Arts Partnership of
Greater Spartanburg, its donors, the County and City of
Spartanburg  and the South Carolina Arts Commission which
receives support from the National Endowment for the Arts and
the John and Susan Bennett Memorial Arts Fund of the Coastal
Community Foundation of South Carolina

Summary and concept: This Story is based on the retelling of
numerous tall tales about Trotting Sally racing and beating steam
powered locomotives.

First Edition

Published by **Hairy Toe Productions**

Trotting Sally was always down at the Union Station Depot in ole Spartanburg Town, always dancing and always playing his fiddle Rosalie. He could make her talk. He'd say, "Rosalie, you hungry?" Then he'd tuck that fiddle under his chin and place the bow on the strings and see-saw out the answer, "Y-E-S!"

"What you want to eat?" he'd ask.

She'd answer, "P-E-A-C-H P-I-E."

Trotting Sally's real name was George Mullins. Legend has it when George was a little boy picking cotton in the fields he saw a horse pulling a carriage along the dusty road. The horse's name was Sally. Little George could run fast so he started trotting alongside the carriage. It wasn't long before he was out in front, and he beat that carriage to town like some kind of greased lighting. From that day on, folks called him Trotting Sally. Sometimes, just like a horse, he would paw the ground and neigh.

One day when Trotting Sally was down at Union Station dancing and playing Rosalie, an old fellow asked, "Trottin' Sally, I hear tell that you are fast on your feet. Why I hear tell that you can outrun horses and even once outran a Tin Lizzie Ford automobile?" Trotting Sally didn't say anything. He just smiled and kept on fiddling.

"I hear tell that you can outrun a locomotive," the old man exclaimed. Another fellow quickly chimed in, "Now that's hard to believe!"
Trotting Sally just kept on playing Rosalie.
"We ought to have a race!" another man declared. "I reckon then we'd know for sure."
"What do you say, Trottin' Sally?" he asked.
Trotting Sally stopped playing, pawed the ground, neighed, and announced, "It is a race that's gonna be, and for sure a race I'm gonna win!"

It seemed everyone came out early the next morning to see the contest between man and machine.

There were folks as far as the eye could see. It was decided that Trotting Sally would race the Carolina Special, a passenger train that ran from Charleston, South Carolina, to Cincinnati, Ohio. It had a scheduled stop in Spartanburg.

The race would begin at Union Station and finish 12 miles down the line at the depot in Inman, South Carolina. As the Carolina Special rolled in, Trotting Sally was already at the station dancing and playing Rosalie. There was so much excitement you could feel it in the air.

When the last ticket was sold, the conductor pulled his pocket watch out and shouted, "ALL ABOARD!"

All eyes were on Trotting Sally when he took off his old hat and handed it to the engineer. "I'll get it back when you get there," he vowed.

Then he trotted over to the starting position at the front of the train.

The sheriff pulled out his pistol, held it high in the air, and bellowed, "Get on your mark, get set ...." BANG!

Now Trotting Sally got off with a lightning quick start. That ole locomotive's wheels screeched with a powerful chug, followed by another, and another, chug-a-lug, chug-a-lug, chug-a-lug!

By the time the Carolina Special got up to speed, Trotting Sally was plum out of sight. Some folks along the railroad tracks said that they could see him coming, but they never saw him pass.

He jumped over Blackstock Road at the fairgrounds, zipped by Hayne's Rail Yard, and darted past Sigsbee's Crossing. He leapt over Lawson's Fork Creek and whooshed past Doc Gibson's place.

The cows mooed, the chickens cackled, and the ole rooster cockle-doodle-dooed as **Trotting Sally** and the **Special** blew by.

At one point it seemed the Carolina Special was about to catch up to him. Trotting Sally just picked up the pace. "He's faster than a dog licking a dish," the brakeman shouted.

When Trotting Sally reached the outskirts of Inman, he leapt onto the tracks. A woman cried out, "There he is!"
A man shouted, "And there's the Special. It's gonna be close!"

Everyone cheered when Trotting Sally reached the depot first. Even the engineer blew his whistle to join in the celebration.

When the train finally came to a screeching halt, the engineer pulled the chain and blew off her steam. WHIZZZZZZZZZZ! Then he reached out and handed Trotting Sally his hat. Trotting Sally put it on his head, pawed the ground, and neighed like a horse! Everyone shouted, "Hip, hip, hooray!"

With a big smile on his face, Trotting Sally swung Rosalie around from his back, tucked her under his chin, and began fiddling. Fiddle-dee and fiddle-dum. Everyone danced. And that's the story of the day Trotting Sally beat the Carolina Special!

# Trotting Sally

George Washington Mullins was born a slave in 1856 on the Oakland Plantation near Greenville, South Carolina. After the civil war his father relocated the family to nearby Spartanburg County. There they settled on farmland where his father had been born and spent his childhood. It was called the Mullins Plantation.

George began playing the fiddle in his late teens or early twenties. His personality sparkled with charming energy as he pulled the bow across the strings. He was a natural entertainer. Legend has it that he got his nickname after outrunning a horse by the name of Sally. From that day on locals called him Trotting Sally.

He married in 1880. He and his wife Lizzie became tenant farmers. They had six children. George also worked other odd jobs to help provide for his growing family. By the turn of the century he was known far and wide as the man who could outwork three men half his age, never tired, and could outrun horses, automobiles, and trains. He seemed to be everywhere, traveling only by foot.

A Trotting Sally sighting was special. He played short street shows, fiddling, dancing, and telling jokes. He often stopped and played with other musicians along the dusty crossroad communities around Spartanburg County and parts of Western North Carolina. One of his favorite spots was the Union Station Depot in Spartanburg where he would entertain travelers for nickels and dimes. Numerous articles were written about Trotting Sally. Even the New York Times (1907) featured a short story about "the man who thinks he is a horse."

Trotting Sally died on September 20, 1931, and is buried in an unmarked grave near Boiling Springs, South Carolina.

Author **Johnny Thomas Fowler** is a professional storyteller, award winning old-time musician and popular radio host from Boiling Springs, South Carolina. He is the author of *Trotting Sally: The Roots and Legacy of a Folk Hero* (Kennedy Free Press). He is a South Carolina Community Scholar, a Jean Laney Harris Folk Heritage Recipient, and a featured subject in the book *Southern Appalachian Storytellers* by Saundra Gerrell Kelly (McFarland). Htp50@yahoo.com

Illustrator **Raymond L. Floyd** is an artist, retired-teacher, and entrepreneur originally from Orangeburg, South Carolina. As a child his mother encouraged him to reach for the stars and follow his dreams. He is a graduate of Claflin College where he studied under Arthur Rose, Leo Twiggs and James McFadden. He received his MAT Degree at the University of South Carolina and went on to work as an art teacher in Spartanburg School District 7. In 1995 Raymond worked as Special-Project Artist for Mattel Toys. His photography is published in the book South of Main (Hub City Press). Raylflo@yahoo.com

Made in the USA
Columbia, SC
28 February 2024

32408364R00020